Pathways of Our Fathers

Two Journeys of

Love, Sacrifice, and Family

by Joseph Bolton

Illustrations by Masami Kiyono

Foreword

The stories you are about to read are true.

Of course, no story told about the past is ever one hundred percent true. Our memories are not reliable. The truth gets jumbled, details forgotten. Nonetheless, facts do not lead to understanding. Left on their own, they are a wordy jumble that in the end tell us nothing and help no one. Our souls yearn for a deeper understanding. We need to peel back the layers in a story and illuminate the reasons things are the way they are. You know what I am saying is true. You feel it too.

This is the story of my great-grandparents Eva and Adelard's lives, as well as the lives of my more distant ancestors Atsena, Ouenta and Annengthon. That's why I have turned a flashlight onto the lives of my great-grandparents and my more distant ancestors. I looked into long forgotten corners to seek the truth of who they were: Eva and Adelard; Atsena, Ouenta, and Annengthon.

It is not enough to know that my great-grandparents Eva and Adelard visited Sainte-Anne-de-Beaupré and left Quebec a month later expecting their first child. Nor would it be enough to know that Atsena, Ouenta and Annengthon were the ancestors of three out of four of my mother's grandparents (all but Eva). And it is never enough to know the names of our ancestors. What we seek to understand is *how the past led to*

We like to think that as individuals, we are unique. However, the aspects of who we are have roots in our family going back generations. Look in the mirror and see your great-uncle or aunt looking back at you. Notice the smile or the twinkle in the eye of your grandmother in the face of your child. But our connections are more than appearances. I know and understand the love of my ancestor Atsena and the love of my great-grandmother Eva, because their love is echoed in the love that my mother and her siblings have had for me.

These answers about ourselves and our place in our families are part of the deepest truth of *The Prayer of Atsena.* Enjoy it, ponder it, reflect on its beautiful illustrations. But be warned that you may find yourself in a different place when you finish it.

At the core of *Frankenstein Cliff: A Father's Love from Strength* are experiences from my own life as well as the life of my father. My father did take my brother and me hiking in the White Mountains when we were small, and that I returned to Frankenstein Cliff in August 2019. But by itself, this information provides scant illumination into my father. Yet, as I stood at the bottom of Frankenstein Cliff, I realized that who my father was as a man were all there in this little adventure.

When you finish *Frankenstein Cliff: A Father's Love from Strength,* you will not know about all of my father's US patents, but you will know of his heroic virtue, his love of the underdog, his sense of fair play, and his love for his children. *Frankenstein Cliff: A Father's Love from Strength* illuminates not only into his life but the quiet lives of fathers everywhere.

No book is created in a vacuum, and I owe a debt to many people who helped make this book happen. My first thanks are to this book's illustrator **Masami Kiyono**. Her illustrations bring these stories to life in a way that my poor words would never be able to do. I am also grateful to my **Aunt Jean** who encouraged me to persevere to the finish line. My thanks to **Uncle Jack** who, as an accomplished author himself, lovingly gave me insight into the hard realities of publishing a book. My **Aunt Annie** and **Uncle Tom** for their early reviews and advice. My **Uncle Dave** who helped me discover the truth I already knew about the title of this book even when I was not consciously aware of it myself. A special mention must go to my **Aunt Phyllis** who loved the story about Atsena. I read it to her while she was in hospice, and she died just before I started this book. I believe that she, **Atsena**, **Adelard** and **Eva** all conspired to get me to tell their stories. Speaking of those in heaven, I want to thank my great **Aunts Rita** and **Florence** and their brother, my grandfather **Roland** and my grandmother **Claire** (Eva's daughter) for sharing our family's stories and helping me understand how I fit into all of it.

My thanks to my daughter **Rachel** for giving me an early edit review. My thanks also go to my wife **Mary** for patiently bearing with all the time and treasure I put into this book. I also want to thank my West Point classmate **Bryan Canter** who gave me solid advice on the challenges of book publishing. My thanks also to Zachary Bos and Cat Dossett for their help in editing and publishing this work. Big thanks for the generosity of **Paul Gorbould** of the **Canadian Broadcasting Corporation** for granting permission to use his stunning photograph of Sainte-Anne-de-Beaupre on the cover. Speaking of Canada, *The Prayer of Atsena* is my love letter to you and especially the **French Canadians** and **First Nations** people of Quebec, Ontario, and Nova Scotia. I have never forgotten the land of my ancestors and part of my heart will always be there.

If you enjoyed this book pass it on to others or even better encourage others to acquire a copy of their own. The world needs positive messages now. As the Canadian rock band Rush wrote in their song "Presto": *radiate more light than heat.*

The Prayer of Atsena

"He will turn the hearts of the fathers to their children, and the hearts of the children to their fathers." Malachi 4:6

COPYRIGHT, 1901,
BY DETROIT PHOTOGRAPHIC CO.

Early evening, Beaupré, Quebec, December 1916:

Atsena dit Du Plat Great Bear Chief of the Huron Wendats stood in the church sanctuary of Sainte-Anne-de-Beaupré, transfixed with awe and love for his son. Adelard was kneeling beside his wife Eva before the statue of Saint Anne. In the quiet light of a flickering candle, Adelard could see Eva's eyes closed, lips moving ever-so slightly in prayer. His own eyes were open and glistening in the dim light. They were kind eyes, patient, and perhaps in a better time playful, but now sadness, not mirth, shone in them. It was those eyes that reminded Atsena most of his beloved daughter, Ouenta.

Adelard was not Atsena's son exactly, but his sixth great-grandson. Nonetheless, he loved him as a son because he was a descendant of his daughter Ouenta. She was gone now, living in the Great Father's Longhouse with his wife Annengthon. But now, kneeling in front of him, was a part of Ouenta still living in this world, and Atsena loved him for it.

Adelard's toolmaker hands, rugged and callused, fidgeted with a black rosary. He would glance at it, twisting and turning a dark bead, then looking up at the statue of Saint Anne. He was careful to not to disturb Eva, only moving his head slightly for an occasional, concerned glimpse at her delicate hands, clenching the rosary intertwined between her fingers. She prayed, pleaded. They have been married for over ten years, and although their marriage was happy, it was not blessed with children.

Neither prayers, novenas, nor candles brought forth new life into their world. Adelard had resigned himself that he would never be a father, and unlike other men, he did not blame Eva. He loved her, and he would do anything to heal her pain.

For Eva, having grown up in the bustle of a French-Canadian family of nine children, the lack of even one child was unbearable. So now they prayed at the church dedicated to Saint Anne, the mother of Mary and the grandmother of Jesus, and she pleaded, mother to mother, woman to woman, for children of her own.

As Atsena watched his son and his wife he became aware of Elder Brother standing beside him. Elder Brother was what the Black Robes said was his guardian angel, given to all people as a special protector by the Great Father. Atsena remembered the first time he saw Elder Brother after he died at the end of a Mohawk warrior's club in the Iroquois village of Canajoharie, two hundred and fifty-nine years ago.

***

Early morning, before the dawn, Canajoharie, August 1657

At that point Atsena had been a prisoner of the Mohawks for a full moon, captured in Quebec by a Mohawk raiding party and forced to march to the Mohawk River far to the south. Enduring ritualistic humiliation and slavery, he was mocked especially for his Christian faith. But the worst suffering was reliving his last memory of Ouenta, not yet a woman, sleeping contently in the arms of Annengthon.

On a moonless night, Atsena sneaked out with the intention to go north and return to Ouenta and Annengthon. But he did not leave unobserved. Mercifully, he was only briefly aware of the pain and a flash of light as the club swung and hit the right side of his temple.

Atsena awoke to find himself face down in the snow. Lifting his head, he saw a middle-aged Wendat man of his tribe sitting beside a crackling fire. Instinct told him he was now in the realm of the dead. And although he did not know the man, his presence felt familiar. Atsena shifted himself to sit by the fire, though no heat seemed to emanate from its flames. Nor did he feel the cold of the snow, for that matter

"I believe I may know you," Atsena said to the man. "May I ask your name?"

"Don't you know me, Atsena? I have always been with you," the man responded. He tossed a few logs in the fire. "The Great Father sent me to you while you were still in your mother's womb."

Atsena lowered his head for a moment, his eyes probing the burning logs, wondering what to say next. He heard none of the usual sounds of the forest: wind, birds, people moving about. Nothing but the crackle of fire.

"Are you now going to take me to the Great Father's Longhouse?" he said finally.

"Yes, but not yet. You are not ready, Atsena, to have your eyes uncovered so you can see the next world. Now we must walk together."

With that the Wendat man rose, smiling, and with his outstretched hand lifted Atsena to his feet. "You may call me Elder Brother."

***

It took two hundred and fifty-nine years to finally reach Quebec north of *Trois- Rivières*. During their journey, Elder Brother shared many things with Atsena about the man's own life, where he helped people and when he failed to follow the way of love toward his fellow human beings. And Atsena saw how he hurt others and how sometimes his actions hurt himself. But Elder Brother remained with him, and as Atsena began to understand his life, he let go of all that kept him from entering the Great Father's Longhouse.

Early evening, Beaupré, Quebec, December 1916:

With the journey finished, Elder Brother announced that Atsena was ready to go the Great Father. But Atsena still had one final question.

"Elder Brother, you told me in our travels together that Ouenta became a woman, took a husband, and had children," Atsena began.

"Yes. Even now they live scattered about this land," Elder Brother responded.

"But of all the people we have seen together, it was never revealed to me which ones were my children," Atsena continued. "On my last day before I go to the Great Father, may I see at least see at least one of them?"

So Elder Brother guided him into the Shrine of Sainte-Anne-de-Beaupré, where Adelard and his wife Eva knelt in front of the statue of Saint Anne.

For a few minutes Elder Brother and Atsena watched Adelard and Eva. Then, placing a hand on Atsena's shoulder, Elder Brother reminded Atsena: "It is a time of joy, my brother; Ouenta and Annengthon await you at the door to the Great Father's Longhouse."

But Atsena paused. "Wait, Elder Brother… My son's wife, Eva, her tears burrow into my heart. What do they pray for?"

"Children, they have no children," he responded. "Now come, Ouenta and Annengthon are waiting for you."

As they turned to leave, the doors of the church heaved open, flooding the nave with an unearthly light, impossibly bright. Atsena could make out the silhouette of two women just outside. It was Ouenta and Annengthon.

"Will their prayer be answered?" he said at last.

But Elder Brother shook his head. "No, Atsena. A child for them will only bring suffering."

Adelard's right hand slowly moved to cover Eva's hands. The Gordian knot of her rosary unwound and fell to the floor as Adelard's fingers entwined with hers. Adelard lifted the rosary and wrapped both their hands with the black wooden beads.

"Elder Brother..." Atsena was mesmerized. Instead of joining Ouenta and Annengthon, he stepped closer to the couple and wiped a tear from Eva's eye. Her eyes closed as a gentle breeze lilted across her cheek.

"Elder Brother," Atsena murmured, "see the love within her---so much love, it's bursting through her tears. She suffers because she loves."

Finally he understood. When he suffered with the loss of watching his child Ouenta grow older, he suffered because he loved. But he would rather have known his daughter for just a few short years and suffer centuries without her than never to have loved at all.

"Elder Brother, you say she will suffer," Atsena said suddenly. "But in this life, Love and Suffering are brothers traveling together. I have seen it these years, wandering with you over the Earth. There is no love without sacrifice, without suffering. It is a poor, miserable human being who has never suffered for love." His gaze turned again to Eva and Adelard. "I join my prayers with my son and his wife. My heart stands with them."

Elder Brother turned to face to Atsena: "Do you know what you are asking, brother?" he asked. "Are you willing to suffer with them? Are you willing to stay with them?"

Atsena smiled. "Yes, Elder Brother, I will stay with them and watch over them," he said resolutely. "I will experience their joys, their sufferings, theirs and their children's."

And then heavy door shut, and darkness returned to the church.

In the candlelight, Elder Brother reached out and drew Atsena into his arms. "I can't stay with you, my brother," he explained. "This journey you must do alone. Even I do not know how long you must remain, but you cannot follow me to the Great Father's Longhouse until one of your children remembers you in their prayers."

And with that Atsena stood alone, unseen, with Adelard and Eva in the Shrine of Sainte-Anne-de-Beaupré.

One hundred years passed. Still, Atsena stayed and watched over his family. He watched with joy the birth of Adelard and Eva's first daughter Vivian, only to watch her pass to the Great Father when she had reached eighteen years of age.

And he rejoiced in the engagement of Adelard and Eva's second daughter, Claire, to Roland. He grieved with Eva when Adelard, too, was taken to the Great Father before their daughter's wedding.

He stayed with Eva and prayed to the Great Father for her, and soon Claire and Roland had a family of their own. And he realized that Eva and Adelard's legacy were as Elder Brother had warned: a life of suffering. Yet they also shared great love and happiness with Eva's eleven grandchildren.

In time Eva joined Adelard with the Great Father. But, as he had promised, Atsena continued to watch their grandchildren and great-grandchildren with a father's love. They were his daughter Ouenta's children, and therefore his children, too.

Early Sunday Morning, Our Lady of the Lake Church, Leominster, Massachusetts September 2019:

Atsena dit Du Plat Great Bear Chief of the Huron Wendats stood in the nave of Our Lady of the Lake, transfixed with awe and love at his son. Today, a great-grandson of Eva and Adelard had remembered his name in the Holy Mass.

Light beamed into the church as it had in the Shrine of Sainte Anne all those years ago. The words of the priest echoed throughout the Our Lady of the Lake: *"Remember also those who have died in the peace of Christ and all the dead, whose faith you alone have known. Especially for Atsena dit Du Plat, Ouenta and Annengthon, for whom this Mass is offered. To all of us, your children, grant, O merciful Father, that we may enter into a heavenly inheritance with the blessed Virgin Mary, Mother of God…"*

At these words, a hand came to rest on Atsena's shoulder. Ouenta and Annengthon stood behind him, and Elder Brother, Adelard and Eva, and Atsena's many children who had passed on to the Great Father's Longhouse. Atsena gazed upon his family, some still in this world, some who had passed on. And, with joy, he stepped through the doorway.

INTÉRIEUR DE LA BASILIQUE - INTERIOR - ST. ANNE DE BEAUPRÉ

Frankenstein Cliff: A Father's Love from Strength

"I will guide you in the way of wisdom and I will lead you in upright paths. When you walk, your steps will not be hampered, and when you run, you will not stumble." Proverbs 4:11-12

In August of 1969, in the days long before cell phones and GPS, a young, athletic, twenty-nine-year-old man stood at bottom of the trail to Frankenstein Cliff in Crawford Notch, New Hampshire. With him were his two sons, ages five and four. The man had grown to love the White Mountains while an engineering student at Northeastern University in Boston, and for many years, he would treasure black-and-white pictures of himself and his college buddies climbing Mount Washington.

The young father loved his boys and wanted to share the adventure of the mountains with them. The older one, named Joey after his father, was inquisitive and curious. Intuitive, he could grasp scientific and mathematical concepts that simultaneously astonished and intimidated adults around him. Joey, though, was forgetful, hated details, couldn't tie his shoes, and struggled with the mundane. The same adults around him, at those times, found Joey exasperating.

The younger boy Davy, nicknamed "Muggsy" by his father, loved to throw rocks. He had an uncanny sense of direction in the woods. Naturally fearless, he always wanted to be the trailblazer on any expedition. His jet-black hair, ruddy cheeks and dark eyes made him irresistible to the adults around him. Muggsy also tended to disappear on his own adventures leaving a trail of broken windows (darn rocks), doors taken off hinges, and other expensive household disasters. It was safe to say, that while Muggsy was irresistibly lovable, the adults around him also found him exasperating, just like his brother. But the young father loved those boys, and that is why he now stood at the trail head of Frankenstein Cliff, in August of 1969.

The father studied the roughly drawn map in front of him, and with Muggsy blazing the trail and Joey at his side asking questions, he entered the woods.

Passing underneath Frankenstein Trestle prompted questions from Joey: When will a train be coming? Will we be OK under the track? Will it smoke? Why do trains smoke? Muggsy looked around for a rock that would fit into his hand.

Leaving the trestle behind, the trail became steep, and the boys scrambled up on all fours. A small rock would occasionally kick lose and tumble down the mountain. The boys should have felt scared, but didn't. Joey and Muggsy trusted their father and felt safe with him. Their father's strength emanated from him, protecting the boys. They always felt invincible within their father's love. As they continued to climb, the father would occasionally reach down and pull up the boys to the next ledge along the trail. Throughout his life, he always had a soft spot for the underdog and would reach out to lift up the vulnerable around him.

At the summit, the little group stopped to rest and enjoy the view of the White Mountains and Crawford Notch stretching below them. Joey had to know the name of every mountain, wanted to know if each had a trail, which mountain was highest and how high it was. Muggsy found a nice rock and tossed it over the side of the cliff, listening for the clatter below.

After a snack, the father led his boys further on the trail past the cliff. Did they miss the turn off loop to the bottom? Did the father overestimate the length of the trail ahead? No one knows, but hours later, the father and his boys found themselves back on the road many miles north of the campground where they were staying. With cell phones still decades in the future, they started the trek south along the road. Surely someone would give them a ride back to the campground. The father turned and stuck his thumb out at every passing car.

But no one gave them a ride. Car after car rode on by the father and his two very young sons. The boys were tired by this time, and their father would alternate with one boy on his shoulders and the other by his side, hand-in-hand. But he never complained, or cursed the drivers, or felt bad for himself. In fact, throughout his whole life, no one heard him say anything negative about anyone. But the father never forgot walking along that road with his boys, mile after mile, when no one gave them a ride. For the rest of his life, as long as he was able, the father would always give a ride to strangers thumbing it on the side of the road. Some of them were blind. One in New Hampshire was a philosophy graduate student. Another was a British man in his twenties touring the country with just a backpack and a deck of cards. Some were just people needing a ride. In any case, the father never passed anyone in need on the road as others had done to him.

***

It was many years later, and the father awoke from an uneasy sleep by a chime beside his bed. His worried thoughts never let him sleep as deeply or as long as he wanted now. The chime rang again, and he struggled to sit up on the side of the bed. He put his glasses on

and looked at the clock: 1:22 AM. The father carefully swung his feet on to the floor and balanced himself.

He slept in the basement and his boy's room was on the second floor, so he readied himself to climb the two flights of stairs. Racked with the illnesses of old age, the man who climbed Mt. Washington years ago now struggled to walk across the room, much less two flights of stairs. But as he did many times over the last few months, the father ascended the stairs to the boy's door.

Cracking the door open, he could see Muggsy's hair by the hall light. His hair was still thick and jet black for his forty-eight years. As the door widened, Muggsy's dark eyes came into view, just barely visible above his full CPAP mask. Relief shone in Muggsy's eyes as he recognized his father. Muggsy could not throw any rocks anymore, much less walk. He could barely move his finger to ring the chime to his father's room. ALS had taken everything from Muggsy, everything but love, and that love emanated from his father at the door.

Muggsy's requests for help came at all hours and quite often more than once a night. Tonight, the father lifted his boy and adjusted his position on the bed. It was tiring, but the father never complained, and he never failed to answer the chime. The old father loved his boy, and that is why he sat beside his bed and held his hand, in August of 2013.

***

Years passed, and Joey now stood alone at the foot of Frankenstein Cliff trail. As he stood there trying to see the cliff from the parking lot, it suddenly occurred to him that he was now old enough to be his father's father when the three of them stood here fifty years ago. This thought quickly led to another: that he was the last person on this Earth who had any firsthand knowledge of what happened that day.

Muggsy had died from ALS in November of 2013, and his father had passed away last January. The memory of that hike suddenly felt fragile. Trying to reclaim it, Joey took a few tentative steps into the forest and stood looking up the trail. He hoped that by standing on the trail and intersecting himself with this place of memory he would also intersect himself with that moment of time fifty years ago…and remember. Alas, no new memories would come. Nevertheless, Joey stood there, remembering his father's love. The father who loved them enough to drive three hours to the White Mountains to camp and take them on an adventure in the woods. Joey loved his father and honored him. And that is why he now stood at the trail head of Frankenstein Cliff, in August of 2019.

Afterword

Artist's Note

My father was my first art teacher. Growing up in one of the small cities hidden around the hills of Northern California, I would watch him draw cartoon characters that were inspired by one of the Japanese animations that he himself watched as a child. While growing up in Tokyo, he was introduced to a collection of movies and comics featuring robot fighters, ninja warriors, etc.

However, he had also learned many older tales that were meant to teach Buddhist ideas such as forgiveness, sacrifice, and the importance of honoring the past. Though my family was not devout, my father made sure I learned these stories. I did not understand them fully at the time, but those fables still come to me, especially when I'm creating art.

Though Joe and I come from very different backgrounds and grew up on opposite sides of the country, there is something universal about wanting to bring life to your history and to remember your family as real people as opposed to names on a page. *The Prayer of Atsena* is also a story with many of the same lessons I had learned from my own culture. Because of that, I wanted to make sure my illustrations honored Atsena's history, Eva's struggles, and the family's faith.

When I wasn't drawing, I spent much of my time on this project conducting research. I have no indigenous blood in my family (as far as I am aware) and know little about the different cultures that originate from the Northeast. This became especially clear to me when Joe pointed out that my early sketches of Atsena made it look like he lived on the plains, instead of a fur-wearing man from Quebec getting ready for winter. (Being a Californian, that last aspect admittedly hadn't crossed my mind until that point.) Joe happily supplied me with more visual references, but I decided to do what I could to learn more about their culture, history, and introduction to Catholicism. Though I still have much to learn, I hope that my depictions of Atsena, Ouenta and Annengthon are respectful and show them as real people, just as I would hope another artist would show my own ancestors.

For this project, I also made sure to take a page from art history. Joe made it clear that Atsena would not use modern iconography to envision his Catholic faith, specifically when it came to his interactions with the angelic figure of Elder Brother. To give Elder Brother an otherworldly presence, I had the idea to look into the halo I had seen in Medieval European artwork. Upon investigation, I realized that such imagery was in no way unique to Europe. This symbol of divinity has been used by multiple religions across the world, ranging from Africa, the Middle East, Rome, and Asia, with the later specifically using it in Buddhist illustration.

Though I feel silly for not remembering something that was likely taught to me in a history class, or for perhaps never making the connection in the first place, it seemed right to find another connection between the past and stories we remember.

- Masami Kiyono

Crédit photo: François-Marie Héraud, Sanctuaire Sainte-Anne-de-Beaupré